P9-CKX-112

The Creepiest Sleepover Ever

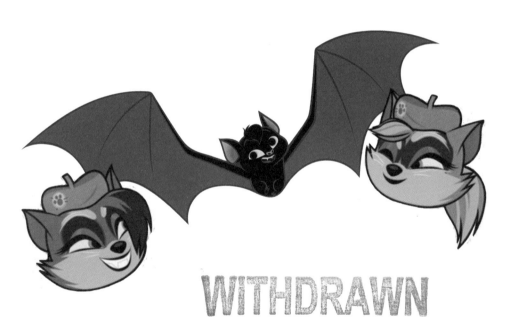

WITHDRAWN

Adapted by **Ximena Hastings**

Ready-to-Read

Simon Spotlight

New York   London   Toronto   Sydney   New Delhi

SIMON SPOTLIGHT
An imprint of Simon & Schuster Children's Publishing Division
1230 Avenue of the Americas, New York, New York 10020
This Simon Spotlight edition July 2019
TM & © 2019 Sony Pictures Animation Inc. All Rights Reserved.
All rights reserved, including the right of reproduction in whole or in part in any form.
SIMON SPOTLIGHT, READY-TO-READ, and colophon are registered trademarks of
Simon & Schuster, Inc.
For information about special discounts for bulk purchases, please contact
Simon & Schuster Special Sales at 1-866-506-1949 or business@simonandschuster.com.
Manufactured in the United States of America 0619 LAK
10 9 8 7 6 5 4 3 2 1
ISBN 978-1-5344-4064-7 (hc)
ISBN 978-1-5344-4063-0 (pbk)
ISBN 978-1-5344-4065-4 (eBook)

There's something creepy happening at
Hotel Transylvania.
Aunt Lydia has discovered footprints!
"I suspect they come from *human*
shoes! They must be spying
on the hotel!" she says.

Aunt Lydia asks Mavis, Pedro, Hank, and Wendy to be on high alert.
"Alert!" chirps Diane the chicken.
Mavis doesn't care about a human attack today, though.
Her friends Sophie and Charlotte from her old Ghoul Guides troop are visiting.

Mavis throws on her Ghoul Guides sash and looks at the door excitedly. "I've got everything planned so we can relive all the fun times!" she exclaims.

Wendy isn't happy.
She doesn't always feel like she's part of the group.

Sophie and Charlotte arrive, and the troop starts their activities.

First, they go bird-watching on the roof, but Wendy struggles with her binoculars and gets picked up by a giant monster!

Later, the girls work on crafts in the restaurant.

Mavis makes a bat hat.

Charlotte and Sophie make cozy scarves.

But Wendy's wool gets stuck on Uncle Gene's ear hair! Yuck!

The ghoul troop goes out to the graveyard to practice archery. Mavis, Charlotte, and Sophie all hit their target, but Wendy misses, and the arrow flies up into the air and lands straight through her!

Charlotte and Sophie are about to leave when suddenly Aunt Lydia puts the hotel on lockdown!

"This. Is. Amazing!" cries Mavis.
"Now we can earn our
Creepover badge and finally
complete our sashes!"

The other girls look nervous, but
Mavis is excited.
"This is going to be the BEST.
CREEPOVER. EVER!"

"Where will we sleep, Mavis?
We can't all share your casket,"
Charlotte asks.
"Of course not, this is a
legit creepover!" Mavis says, pointing
to the tent she has set up in her room.

The werewolves decide to check out the tent.
They tear it to pieces with their claws!
"Guess we'll need our own room," they say innocently.
Then they leave and go to a new bedroom for the night.

Meanwhile, Mavis and Wendy share
the casket and try to get some
sleep. It doesn't last long.
A loud alarm rings all over
the hotel. Mavis and Wendy jump
out of the casket and run to the lobby.

Aunt Lydia has found a crossword puzzle and a pencil.
Human stuff!

Everyone is scared.

They can't believe there's an actual human at the hotel.

Mavis notices Charlotte and Sophie are not in the lobby—they could be in danger!

Mavis and Wendy run to Charlotte
and Sophie's room and push
the door down.

When Mavis looks up, she sees that
Charlotte and Sophie are the humans
at the hotel!
Everyone screams!

"I always thought werewolves turning into humans was just a myth," Wendy says as she inspects Charlotte's face.

"So this is why you never wanted to have a creepover party . . . you didn't want anyone to know you're human," Mavis says.

"Aren't you guys scared of us?"
asks Sophie.
"No, but being caught with humans
in the hotel by Aunt Lydia
is something to be scared of!"
Mavis says.

Aunt Lydia's goons suddenly appear in
the hallway.
They are searching every room for
the human.

The ghoul troop quickly hides.

"What do we do? We won't
turn back to werewolves until
nightfall!" Charlotte exclaims.
"Good thing we're expert Ghoul Guides
then, right? We'll use our survival
skills to escape," Mavis says.

Mavis has the perfect idea: She'll hide Charlotte and Sophie in a guard's suit.

Meanwhile, the goons are still searching for the human in every swamp, graveyard, haunted house, and henhouse in sight.

The ghoul troop decides to go to a room that's already been searched. They are creeping along the hallway . . .

when they are spotted by
Aunt Lydia!
"Mavis, stop!" Aunt Lydia demands.

"Run!" Mavis screams.
But Charlotte and Sophie can't move
fast enough in the suit.

Mavis turns into a bat and tries
pushing them forward.
Aunt Lydia is getting closer . . . and
closer . . . and closer.

The girls still aren't moving!
"It's hero time," Wendy says.
Wendy jumps into the air and
catches the sisters in her blob!

They bounce into the lobby,
but are closely followed by
Aunt Lydia's goons.

"What is going on?!" asks Aunt Lydia.
Aunt Lydia sniffs the suit.
"Is that . . . *human*?!" she shrieks.
"You." She points her finger at Pedro.
"Open it!"

Pedro opens the suit to reveal . . .

the sisters back in their werewolf form!
Aunt Lydia shrugs and continues her
search on the roof.

"That was super close! You really saved the day, Wendy," Charlotte says. "You really are a true friend," Mavis says.

Wendy smiles. She finally feels like she's part of the ghoul troop.

They all giggle and wonder where
the human stuff came from. . . .

It's Diane the chicken's!